1

is.
ca
by

A Nod from Nelson

A Nod from Nelson

SIMON WESTON
in collaboration with David FitzGerald

Illustrated by
Jac Jones

P o n t

To the real Mike the Milk – he knows who he is –
for inspiring *A Nod from Nelson*. S.W.

In memory of Camilla Pisani and her love of horses. D.F.

Published in 2008 by Pont Books, an imprint of
Gomer Press, Llandysul, Ceredigion, SA44 4JL

ISBN 978 1 84323 813 3
A CIP record for this title is available from the British Library.

This book is published with the financial support of the
Welsh Books Council.

Printed and bound in Wales at
Gomer Press, Llandysul, Ceredigion

Chapter One

Hello! There you are! I was wondering when you were coming in. Allow me to introduce myself. My name is Nelson, Nelson the 'orse . . . sorry, h-h-h-orse. Mammy always told me to pronounce my aitches properly.

Welcome to my stable at the back of the St Mary Dairy in Pont-y-cary, a stable which I share with a couple of rats. Within the old stone walls, we all get along just fine, living happily together under a shiny Welsh slate roof, proof that anyone can stay friends if they try hard enough. Oh, and Cardigan lives next door as well. He was a racehorse – that's why we call him Cardigan – he was a *jumper* you see! Raced against the best, mind you! 'Desert Orchid' (not his real name of course) sent him a Christmas card for years.

Now I expect you're wondering why I'm here. Well, I used to be the last horse in Wales to pull a milk float. Famous I was. But now I've got . . . retirement. Oh, it's nothing serious; the vet hasn't been and stuck needles in my bum; retirement just means eating oats and sleeping lots and doing the crossword, which isn't easy with hooves. It also means that I've got

time to tell you all the latest news. It's been a real laugh. Come close and settle yourself down, and I'll tell you all about it . . .

It was last Saturday morning – no, Sunday – no, hang on, Saturday, because Cardiff played Plymouth away from home. Mike the Milk – that's my owner – had just taken delivery of Floatie! Floatie is my replacement, a motorised milk float, all bumpers and bits and, get this, *electric*! He runs off a huge battery.

I was giving him the once-over, checking out all those levers and buttons, when the two rats, Rhodri and Rhys, came and balanced on the door beside me.

'Is it working?' squeaked Rhodri.

'No,' I said. 'No, not yet. Mike's gone to fetch a big barrel of oil for the motor.'

With that, Mike staggered back and lifted Floatie's bonnet.

'He's running late!' said Rhys, looking at the big clock that hangs on the wall of the dairy. The hands pointed to ten past five.

'Yes,' I said. 'He's running late and, with all that fussing over the oil, I bet he's forgotten to load enough milk bottles for the round.'

Mike stopped for a moment, scratched his moustache, gave us a little wave and shut the bonnet. Dumping the barrel by the back door of the house, he jumped in and switched on the engine. Floatie's lights flickered and shone. Mike grabbed the steering wheel but he must have pressed his foot down too hard on the accelerator because, suddenly, Floatie shot forward! All the milk crates rattled alarmingly and Floatie came to a shuddering halt.

Mike spent a long time studying the dashboard before starting the engine again. This time Floatie shot backwards – with a fresh rattling of crates and a clattering of milk bottles.

'Not exactly Lewis Hamilton, is he?' said Rhys.

Mike grinned at us and gave a thumbs-up sign. I waved my hoof, wished him luck and then watched him reverse – straight into the barrel of oil. There was a whacking great crunch and Mike's voice shattered the early morning air. 'Oh, yoghurts!' he said, pressing buttons, flicking switches and scratching his head. He must have finally found the forward gear because, all of a sudden, he was off, hurtling through the gates and into the early morning stillness.

Well, Rhys and Rhodri rolled off the door frame, they were laughing so much. I must admit I was grinning myself.

'How fast does that thing go, Nelson?' said Rhys, wiping the tears from his eyes with his tail.

'Oh, pretty fast,' I said. 'About thirty miles an hour. That's what Mike says, anyway.'

'Wow!' said Rhodri. 'That's really, really fast.'

'Nonsense,' said a voice. It came from nowhere.

We all looked at each other.

'Did you hear someone speak?' I said.

'Yes!' said the rats, their eyes darting left and right.

'Where's it coming from?' I said.

'Dunno,' said Rhys. 'Perhaps we've got rats?'

'Yes,' I said. 'You two!'

'Oh, of course!' said Rhodri, shaking his head. 'There's ridiculous I am!'

The voice spoke again. 'You're all talking nonsense, blithering nonsense. Thirty miles an hour is not fast!'

There was a fluttering and a feather or two, and a thin grey pigeon appeared from the rafters above my head and rested on the edge of the door.

'And good morning to you too,' I said. 'Rather personal in your comments, aren't you? Rather rude, even?'

'Sorry,' he said in a very lah-di-dah voice. 'Speak my mind, don't you know. One has to in Her Majesty's Services. Life and death, that sort of thing, what . . . what!'

The rats looked at each other and then at me. 'Is it Comic Relief?' said Rhys to nobody in particular. 'Is he trying to be funny?'

'Shush!' I said. I didn't want to hurt the pigeon's feelings.

'Thirty miles an hour isn't very fast!' he repeated, taking no notice of Rhys's comment.

'I think it's Comic Relief tomorrow,' said Rhodri. 'That pigeon's just turned up a day early.'

'Now *you're* being rude,' I said. 'And two rudes don't make a right, as my mammy used to say.'

The rats shuffled their paws and said they were sorry.

I cleared my throat and spoke directly to the newcomer. 'Anyhow, who are you?'

The pigeon saluted me with his wing and said, 'Can only give my name, rank and number.'

We all looked at him and waited.

'Oh, right,' he said at last. 'That's what you're waiting for, aren't you, my name, rank and number . . .?'

I began to wonder if I should go back to my nice comfortable straw and wake up again when he'd sorted himself out.

'Pigeon,' he said. 'Flight Lieutenant, 24556695, retired, sir!'

'Oh, right,' I said. 'Welcome to the St Mary Dairy, Pont-y-cary, Pigeon, Flight Lieutenant, 24556695, retired. I'm . . . Nelson, milk horse, 01 572 265486, leave a message if I'm not in.' I saluted with my hoof and the rats giggled. 'And tell me why, Flight Lieutenant, were we talking nonsense?'

'Because thirty really isn't fast . . .' he repeated, puffing out his chest. 'Some pigeons go a lot faster.'

'Not with two hundred bottles of milk and forty yoghurts on their back!' I pointed out.

He looked a little lost for words and was about to open his beak when I said, 'Anyway, what are you doing here?'

'Can't tell you that. Top secret. On a mission. France.'

'France?' I said.

The pigeon looked round nervously. 'Who told you that? That's top secret.'

'*You* just did,' I said.

'Did I?' He slumped down on his little legs and gave a big sigh. 'Oh, rats,' he said and then turned to Rhodri and Rhys. 'No offence, gentlemen! It looks like I'm lost again.' He sniffed and I knew that the little fellow was in trouble.

'Don't worry,' said Rhys. 'You've landed at the St Mary Dairy in Pont-y-cary, where we look after everyone.'

'Even lost pigeons!' added Rhodri.

Something told me that this was going to be a long day, a very, very long day.

Chapter Two

There you are. I'm glad you're back. I thought for a moment I wasn't going to see you again! I was telling you about Flight Lieutenant Pigeon, 24556695, retired, wasn't I?

I have to say that he was a bit of a potty pigeon and a bit off course, but I felt sorry for him so I said he could stay. He found a perch in the stable and nodded off just in time to miss the duckling chorus. The quacking in the reeds around the pond could only mean one thing. Sir Francis Drake and his team of rugby-playing ducklings were up, and about to start their early-morning training.

The reeds parted and there they stood, Duck Rugby's finest team, the *All Quacks*. They've only ever lost once, to a bunch of sheep, the *Baaaa-barians*!

'Right,' said Sir Francis. 'Three circuits of the pond and no talking to the horse. I want to see work, work . . . work!'

Every morning it's the same. No talking to the horse. He thinks he's better than everyone, does our Sir Francis. He's a right stuck-up duck and there's nothing worse than a stuck-up duck, unless it's an unpleasant pheasant! Now they can be really nasty.

Off went the *All Quacks* for a pre-season warm-up waddle and things went quiet again, well, for about thirty seconds. Suddenly there was complete commotion. I could hear quacking and flapping and Sir Francis's booming voice: 'Look out! . . . careful! . . . it's all over my feathers! . . . what idiot did this?' Honestly, the noise that some creatures make.

Slowly back through the early-morning light came Sir Francis and his ducklings, or rather, should I say 'mucklings'? They were filthy. Even at a distance, I could see their feathers were all spattered in mud. But as the mucklings waddled closer to my stable, I could see it was . . . oil. OIL!

'Some idiot,' spluttered Sir Francis. 'Some idiot has spilt oil all over my training ground! I have just had a very nasty nine-duck pile-up!'

I looked at the state of the feathered forwards and then shouted for

Rhodri and Rhys. 'Better let yourselves into Mike's kitchen, lads. Get some washing-up liquid and quick!'

The rats looked confused. 'Are we doing the dishes?' asked Rhodri. 'Again?'

'No. The ducks!' I said. 'Detergent gets oil off feathers and we need to get that oil off as quickly as possible.'

The rats shot off to find some washing-up liquid. Sir Francis stood there dripping.

'You've had a bit of an oil spill, I see,' I said.

'Yes!' he said, sounding really unhappy.

'*Duckhams?*'

'Very funny,' he said, wiping his bill with his wing and beginning to look angry. 'Who could have done this?'

'Well, I might be able to help you there. Mike has got a brand-new milk float and I think he was filling up with oil just before he went off on his round. Had a bit of an accident with the barrel, knocked it over, backed into it, he did! It must have sprung a leak.'

Just at that moment Rhodri and Rhys came staggering back, carrying a big bottle of washing-up liquid. I told them to stick it over by the stable tap and then, leaning over the door, I drew back the bolt with my teeth. Now . . . please don't tell anyone that I can do that, especially Mike! Mike hasn't got a clue that I've been letting myself out of my stable for years; he thinks that he forgets to shut the door. That's our little secret, right?

Anyway, the rats put the washing-up liquid on its side by the tap and I went over to help.

'Rhodri, you turn on the tap and, Rhys, when I say . . . *now*! . . . jump on the bottle. Sir Francis, get a duckling and put him under the water.'

Sir Francis waddled off, and waddled back with something small and sticky. It was the outside half! Coated head to foot, he was.

'Right!' I ordered. 'Under the water you go and, Rhys . . . jump now!'

Rhys jumped on the bottle and a squirt of liquid hit 'small and sticky' right on his bill. The duckling shook himself and started to wash.

'Now, mind you dry yourself off properly,' I warned. 'Those feathers need to be good and dry or you won't be able to swim! OK, Sir Francis, who's next?'

Soon the entire team lay in one big puddle of bubbles. There was squirting and scrubbing and quacking and flapping, and more scrubbing and squirting. They were actually enjoying it and started singing songs . . . rugby songs! Well, some of them were really rude! Disgraceful it was.

'Right, Sir Francis, it's your turn,' I said.

'I don't think there's any more liquid left,' said Rhys, jumping up and down on the bottle.

'Rubbish, there's always a little bit left at the bottom. Let me try.'

I stamped on the end with my hoof and, like a bullet, the top of the bottle shot off!

'Duck!' I shouted, hoping that Sir Francis would understand what he was supposed to do. Stupid really, all he did was turn round, the silly drake! The washing-up liquid hit him smack on the bill and knocked him straight into the puddle of bubbles. To make matters worse, just as he was getting up, what was left of the liquid landed on his head! All the ducklings fell about laughing and that just made Sir Francis even angrier. He got to his feet and was about to open his beak and say something really rude when he started to sniff.

'What is that smell?' he said.

I sniffed; Rhodri and Rhys sniffed; all the ducklings sniffed. I had noticed it earlier but hadn't said anything. I then looked at the bottle of washing-up liquid and read the label . . . 'LEMON FRESH'!

'Oh, no!' I said. 'It should have been unperfumed.'

All the ducklings started to sniff one another. 'We smell like sherbet!'

'We can't run onto the rugby field like this!' said Sir Francis, ruffling his feathers to get rid of the smell and the damp. All the ducklings did the same. They shook and they ruffled and they flapped their tiny wings and, one by one, they all went fluffy . . . like dandelion clocks.

'I don't know about the *All Quacks*,' said Rhys. 'You should change your name to the *Sherbet Dips*!'

It was at this point that a small, but very posh voice came from the reeds and stopped everyone in their tracks. 'Excuse me!'

A frog in a tiny black bow tie was sitting on the bank. 'The name's Pond, James Pond,' he said. 'There's something I think you should know about that oil.'

Chapter Three

It's not often you get a talking frog who thinks he's part of the Secret Service. Then again you don't get a lot of rugby-playing ducks either. But that's the beauty of the St Mary Dairy in Pont-y-cary – anything can happen and everyone is welcome, no matter how crazy they are!

James Pond was a bit of a mystery, I must admit. I had never met him before! He said he had been in our pond for years, undercover; that's why I had never seen him. He seemed quite nice really but what he had to tell me was alarming.

'Have you seen where that oil's going?' he said.

'No,' I said, because I hadn't.

He hopped over to the side of the water and I trotted after him. He pointed a flipper at the black puddle that was beginning to form a little river. 'If my calculations are right, the oil will be in the pond in less than fifteen minutes,' he said.

My mouth fell open. He was right. The water would be poisoned.

James Pond turned back to me. Looking up, he said, 'You look shaken. Just like a cocktail! Shaken, not stirred.'

I was well and truly shaken, I must admit. For a moment I couldn't think of what to do and then it came to me. 'We are going to have to build a dam. If we can stop it reaching the pond until Mike comes home, he can clear it up properly. We need twigs and earth and bits of wood and stones.' I looked for the ducklings and Rhodri and Rhys. 'Come on, you guys. Hurry!'

Within a matter of moments, I was surrounded by ducks and rats eager to hear my plan. James Pond sat beside me, nodding and saying things like . . . 'splendid', 'superb' and 'smashing'.

'Who's the frog?' whispered Rhys to me when I stopped to think for a moment.

'His name is Pond, James Pond.'

'Oh!' said Rhys. 'Is he special, then?'

'Yes,' I replied. 'At least he thinks he is. Personally, I think he's watched too many 007 films.' I changed the subject. 'We'll have to form a queue.'

'Arr, Q!' said James, obviously still thinking about the world of films. 'Great man to work with.'

'Grr,' said Rhys. 'Another one with grand ideas!'

'Quite,' I said. 'Now then, start nibbling at those reeds. Let's get on with forming a queue . . .'

'Arr,' repeated the frog. 'Q, great man to work with!'

'Is he related to the pigeon?' asked Rhodri.

'Perhaps he's got a short memory,' said Rhys.

'Quiet!' I said. 'We'll form a chain: you two, nibble through the reeds and the ducks can drop the stalks in front of the oil. Then we'll have to start scraping up the mud and anything else that can help to make a wall.'

I was hoping that Mike would come back any minute. There wasn't a lot I could do with a pair of hooves.

Everybody started to work. The ducks formed a line and the rats started nibbling at the reeds. One by one, each of the long stalks came crashing down and a duckling picked it up and passed it on. From Prop to Back Row to Scrum Half, it was perfect passing, great rugby practice. Even Sir Francis had to agree.

Meanwhile, James Pond was staring into the water, and tutting.

'What's up?' I said.

'It's the newts. They look very scared,' he said, peering into the depths of the pond.

Newts! I thought. I didn't know we had newts. I stared into the water and there, near the edge, about six inches under some weed, were five little faces. 'Well I never! I haven't seen newts in there before!'

'I'm not surprised. They're quite shy,' said James. 'They don't come out much and, of course, newts can't speak, so you'll never hear them.'

'They're *mute* newts!' I said.

'Oh, yes,' said James. 'But they have lovely little faces.'

'Cute, mute newts,' I said. 'Well I never did.'

'They are very scared,' said James. 'I've tried telling them that they are safe, that we are working as quickly as we can.'

I looked at the growing dam. The ducks were passing leaves and reeds and rocks and sticks along the line and Sir Francis was piling everything up, but as fast as they worked, the oil was seeping closer and closer. 'Tell the newts they are going to be fine,' I said and crossed my hooves.

The oil had reached the first of the reeds and was slowly starting to seep up the side of the mud wall. The ducks looked at each other; Rhodri and Rhys looked at each other; James Pond glanced at his newt friends and gave them a smile. 'Everything's going to be all right,' he said reassuringly.

'Any change?' I said.

'No,' said James. 'They still look pretty scared.'

The oil had reached the mud dam and was forming a big dark puddle. The ducks all moved back from the dam and held their breath. Sir Francis crossed his wing feathers and looked at me. 'What happens if it doesn't work?' he said.

I didn't answer him. It had to work; it must work. Where was Mike when I needed him?

I looked at James Pond again. 'Any change?'

'No,' said James. 'No sign of oil in the water, but the newts are still terribly frightened.'

The oil reached the top of the dam . . . and stopped! We all waited but nothing happened. We waited some more and more nothing happened.

Suddenly the ducks all started to clap and quack. Rhodri and Rhys linked paws and began to dance. 'We've done it!' they cheered.

'Tell the newts they're safe,' I said. 'We've stopped the oil.'

James muttered something into the pond and gave a little thumbs-up sign, well, flipper-up really, as frogs don't have thumbs. 'But they're still scared that something might go wrong,' he said.

'No change there then!'

'No, not really,' he said. 'But then what do you expect? How much *change* can you get out of . . . *five pond newts!*'

He started to laugh. The ducks laughed; Sir Francis and Rhodri and Rhys laughed.

'*Five pond newts!*' repeated the frog. '*Change from five pond newts!*'

I didn't think it was especially funny the first time. 'Look,' I said. 'We need to find Mike and quick. Who can go and get him?'

It was then that I heard the voice.

'Flight Lieutenant Pigeon, 24556695, retired, at your service, sir!'

Chapter Four

Well, what could I do? He was so keen and, to be honest, I thought it might just work. Send the pigeon. What a brilliant idea! So I started to explain the route that Mike takes on his milk round. Down Brynteg Lane and into James Street. Then left into Stewart Road and along Caitlin Avenue. Simple! But Flight Lieutenant Pigeon went a bit cross-eyed as I gave him the directions and then his little shoulders started to sag and I realised there must be a big problem. Tiny tears welled up in his eyes and dripped off the end of his beak.

'I'm sorry,' he said. 'I don't think I can do it!'

'What's up?' I could see the little chap was really upset.

He sniffed and said, 'I've got a terrible secret.'

I shuffled my hooves. I wasn't sure what he was going to say.

'It's the most embarrassing thing a pigeon can admit to,' he said.

'You're not a Swansea fan, are you?'

'No,' he said. 'It's worse than that.'

'Manchester United?'

'No . . . not that bad. You see . . . I've lost my sense of direction.'

Well, I sat down. I was speechless. It's like a duck not knowing how to swim, or a horse not knowing how to chew oats!

He started to tell me his story. 'I'm not retired,' he said. 'I just went out on a mission and never found my way home again.'

I tried to cheer him up. 'These things happen. I expect it's just a slight hiccup. You'll feel better after a good rest. When did this happen?'

'Three years ago!'

'Oh!' I said.

'I went out to deliver a message to . . . somebody, I've forgotten . . . at . . . at . . . well, I can't remember where actually . . . so I thought I better go back to the base . . . but I'm not exactly sure where the base was either. I think it began with an M.'

'Arr, M, good man to work with,' said James Pond.

The morning was getting worse by the minute! Then I had an idea. 'Look, why not just fly in circles. I bet you're good at that!'

The pigeon looked at me and sniffed back a tear. 'I've done a lot of that!' he admitted.

'That's perfect then,' I said. 'Fly round the yard and then do it again, only in a slightly bigger circle. Then do it again in a bigger circle and then a bigger one. As long as you can see the roof of my stable, you won't get lost. Just look for a milk float and then circle back and tell us where it is!'

All the ducks clapped and quacked, which was nice. I took a bow. To be honest, I thought I deserved it as it was a clever idea.

'I'll do it,' said Flight Lieutenant Pigeon, and fluttered up to the stable roof. 'I'll keep the stable to my left and look for the milk float on the right. Or the milk float on my left and the stable on my right. No, the stable on my left . . .!'

He flapped into the air, muttering, 'Stable on the left, float on the right . . . stable on the left, float on the right.' He started to circle the yard. He flew around a second time, a bit further away, but we could all still hear him: 'Stable on the left, float on the right.'

'You're doing great!' I shouted.

The rest of the yard looked at me with doubtful faces.

The pigeon flew over for a third time. 'Fable on the left, stoat on the right! No . . . no, table on the left, boat on the right.'

'That's the last we see of him!' said Rhodri.

'Couldn't he take the frog with him?' said Rhys.

I gave them one of my dark glances. 'Listen, you two. If you want to be helpful, go and wake Cardigan. He might be able to help us.' I looked up and the pigeon was gone.

Cardigan's old brown face appeared over the stable door. 'What's happening?'

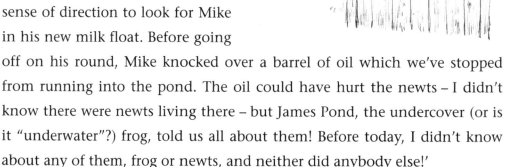

Well, I didn't really know where to start. I took a deep breath. 'We've just sent a pigeon with no sense of direction to look for Mike in his new milk float. Before going off on his round, Mike knocked over a barrel of oil which we've stopped from running into the pond. The oil could have hurt the newts – I didn't know there were newts living there – but James Pond, the undercover (or is it "underwater"?) frog, told us all about them! Before today, I didn't know about any of them, frog or newts, and neither did anybody else!'

Cardigan blinked.

'We need help,' I said.

'You need a vet,' said Cardigan. 'And a holiday!'

I tried to fill in as much detail as possible, and Cardigan listened. He looked at the dam, then at the ducks, then at Rhodri and Rhys and finally at James Pond.

'What can I do to help?' he said.

I scratched my head with my hoof. 'I don't know at the moment but just stay awake and look alert!'

We all waited and waited. The ducks looked at the sky. James looked at the newts. Rhodri and Rhys looked at the dam and I looked at Cardigan. Cardigan just yawned and rested his head on the top of the stable door.

It must have been all of half an hour before I heard some fluttering and Flight Lieutenant Pigeon flopped back into the yard.

'I made it,' he shouted. 'I did what you said, flew round and round, and I made it.'

Everybody clapped. Everybody but Rhodri! He handed Rhys a pound coin. I don't allow betting in my stable so I'm not sure what was going on between them. Anyway, we gave the pigeon time to get his breath back and then I asked him, 'Did you see the milk float?'

'Yes!'

'Where?'

'Stewart Road,' came the reply. 'I landed to check the street name just to make sure.'

'Great,' I said.

'He's broken down,' said the pigeon.

'BUM!'

'The float has got its bonnet up!'

'Double bum!'

I'm not a horse for swearing but there are times and this was one of those times. Just when I thought things were starting to get better, this had to happen. I looked around the yard and all the faces looked back at me.

'Cardigan,' I said. 'How do you fancy going for a little trot?'

He opened one eye. 'You want me to go and get Mike, don't you?'

I smiled at him. He's a clever old horse. 'Just find him and lead him back. It shouldn't be too much trouble. As soon as Mike sees you, he'll panic, think you've got out of your stable, and bring you back again. All you've got to do is let him ride you home – and Bob's your uncle.'

Cardigan nodded. He had got out before and Mike had brought him home immediately. The plan was bound to work. He slid back the bolt on his door and pushed it open. (That was something I had taught him.) He stood in the doorway to the yard and looked left and right. 'Stewart Road?' he said. 'The one with the chippy in it?'

'Yes!' I said. 'The one with the chippy and the broken-down milk float!'

'Oh, yes,' said Cardigan and off he trotted.

Chapter Five

The sound of Cardigan's hooves rattling on the road soon faded and we all looked at each other and wondered what would happen next.

It wasn't good!

A slow blub! . . . blub! . . . blub! sound seemed to be coming from Sir Francis Drake. Surely he wasn't crying? We all looked at him. 'It's not me!' he said and stood back from the small mound of leaves, earth and reeds behind him. The noise happened again. Blub! . . . blub! . . . blub!

James Pond pointed a flipper and in a high-pitched croak cried, 'Look, look at the wall of the dam. It's breaking!'

We all crowded round. Some of the twigs had already given way and bubbles of air were appearing in the oil, as slowly, very slowly, it began to seep between the mud and the leaves and the stones.

'Quick,' I said. 'Get some more earth. Pile it up. See if you can find any more . . . any more . . . anything!'

The whole yard was running in all directions. Ducklings were dragging out bedding from the stable and piling it up in front of the black snake-like puddle creeping ever closer to the pond. The rats started to gnaw at the last

of the reeds while Sir Francis and I scraped away at the earth around the waterside, trying to build up enough of a bank to stop the oil.

'It's no good!' said James Pond. 'It's nearly at the water's edge. We will have to get the newts out.'

I looked at him. 'Can newts live out of water?'

'Of course!' he said. 'They are amphibians, like me! They live on land in the autumn and winter anyway!'

'They do what?' I couldn't believe it.

'They come out of their ponds,' he repeated. 'They *can* walk, you know.'

'Newts go on walking holidays in the autumn and winter?'

James looked at me. 'Not exactly hiking and skiing, no. But newts leave the water when it gets colder and move back in when it's warmer . . . they might not be able to speak but they're not totally stupid.'

It crossed my mind that the newts could have got out of the water as soon as they realised there was a problem, but I suppose they were just too frightened to move. By now the oil had reached the second barrier and was beginning to run along the small bank of earth and reeds. I watched in horror as the black mess started to swallow everything in its path. Why couldn't have Mike been more careful!

James Pond stuck his head in the water and seemed to be talking to the newts. After about a minute, all five of them started to swim to the far bank of the pond and, one by one, they clambered out onto the land. They weren't too stable on their feet but they stepped out onto the yard and stood there blinking at us.

'They will need to be kept wet!' said James. 'Get them over to the tap by the stable. They can stand under it for a while.'

Sir Francis and the ducklings started to guide the five little creatures across the yard towards the tap. The newts were slow and stumbled a lot and it seemed to take forever.

One fell over, right beside Rhys. He helped it up and it staggered off on its way.

'He looks very unsteady!' said Rhodri.

'They don't usually come out till autumn,' I said.

Rhys nodded. 'Probably too early for them! Perhaps they're weak from lack of food. They might need to find something *nutritious*. *Newt-ritious*? Get it?'

Suddenly there was a clatter of hooves in the yard and there stood Cardigan. Sitting on his back, puffing and panting, and looking very red in the face, was Mike. It was difficult to tell which of them looked more out of breath.

'What's going on?' Mike gasped, sliding from Cardigan's back. He looked at the scene. There were: five newts apparently having a shower! a frog wearing a bow tie! a pigeon standing to attention, and a group of lemon-scented ducks huddling by a big pool of oil! 'Problems?' he asked.

'No,' I said. 'We're having a fancy-dress party and we didn't want to leave you out!' Mike can be a bit slow at times. 'Of course there's a problem! Look at the oil.'

Mike's eyes grew wide and his mouth fell open. 'Which idiot did that?' he said.

'YOU!' we all shouted.

For a moment he didn't seem to know what to do, and then he clicked his fingers. 'Wait there!' he yelled and shot off to the shed by the back door, scattering ducks everywhere. Spades and rakes, buckets and old crates came tumbling out. Finally he appeared with a big bag of . . . well, I wasn't sure what it was at first.

He started to drag it over the side of the pond. Rhodri and Rhys ran over to help him, shoving for all they were worth.

'Stand back,' Mike shouted and struggled to lift . . . whatever it was. Suddenly . . . wallop! The top of the bag burst open and he dumped a huge pile of golden sand smack on the edge of the oil. The black sticky mess started to ooze into the sand, turning it a murky grey. Slowly the puddle started to vanish. Then, grabbing a spade, Mike began to scrape back the porridge-like mess. The pond was saved.

Well, I've never seen ducklings do cartwheels before! Rhodri and Rhys did the rumba and even Cardigan hopped about on his old hooves. The newts did nothing, just blinked and shook themselves under the tap, but

I'm sure they were smiling. Mike sat down at the edge of the pond and took off his cap. He scratched his moustache and looked at me. 'What have I done?' he said.

I started to tell him about the crash into the oil drum and then the arrival of Flight Lieutenant Pigeon and then James Pond and the newts and the building of the dam. I told him how we had all worked together and that every one of us had helped to save the pond from being destroyed.

'You've had a busy morning,' he said. 'But at least we have made some new friends.'

I shook my head. There are easier ways, I thought, but I knew what he meant.

Chapter Six

It took some time to clear up, but soon the old yard at the centre of the St Mary Dairy in Pont-y-cary began to look like itself once again.

All the oil was scraped up with the sand and placed in big bags. Then, together with the oil drum, everything was put back into Mike's shed. He would take the lot to the Pen-y-graig tip later on in the day: the men up there would know how to deal with it.

Sir Francis and the ducklings started their training again but soon stopped when the sun grew too hot for them. They went for a swim instead, and why not! That's what the pond was for!

Rhodri and Rhys yawned and scratched and made a nest at the back of my stable in what little straw was left after the building of the dams. They soon fell asleep.

I asked Flight Lieutenant Pigeon if he would like to stay with us for a while and he said 'yes'.

'I'll take first watch in the rafters,' he said and fluttered up into the old wooden beams and promptly started to snore.

The newts staggered back to their watery home and Cardigan turned off the old tap by the barn and said goodnight. 'Wake me up for lunch, will you?' he said.

The milk yard was quiet again.

'Well,' I said. 'What an exciting morning!'

Mike nodded. 'I had no idea I had caused so much trouble. I'm just not used to Floatie yet. All those gears and knobs and buttons! Then there's the battery to be charged. I don't think I did that properly either, which is why it's broken down. And as for the oil spill . . . that was unforgivable. It was so much easier with you, Nelson.' He patted me on the nose. 'All I had to do with you was slip on the harness, shove oats in a bag and away we went.'

'True,' I said. 'There were no mechanical problems with me. No oil needed, no batteries, no lights or brakes, just plain horse power.'

'You backfired a couple of times,' said Mike, rather rudely in my opinion. 'That was the only problem with you.'

'It was the oats; you would keep buying me cheap oats; they give me wind!' I protested.

'Everything gives you wind, Nelson! Apples give you wind; carrots give you wind; wind gives you wind,' said Mike, laughing.

I was about to protest at this outrageous personal attack when I suddenly remembered something . . . something very important.

'Tell me,' I said. 'What makes a really good milkman?'

Mike scratched his moustache and wrinkled his face. 'I'm glad you asked me that,' he said. 'There are so many, many qualities. There is knowing when to walk on tippy-toe so you don't wake people up. There's remembering not to rattle the bottles in their crates . . . oh, and always, always getting the orders right. It's no good leaving semi-skimmed when the family wants full-cream. Orange juice is not the same as grapefruit juice and eggs are not the same as yoghurts. If you get the orders wrong, breakfast is ruined, and breakfast is the most important meal of the day.'

He finished his little lecture and I nodded and fell silent for a while. 'People will be having breakfast right now, I suppose!'

'Yep!' he said. 'Start the day properly with a good breakfast and the rest of the day will sort itself out.'

'So, actually getting the bottles onto the doorstep and making sure everybody on the round has milk to put on their cornflakes and make tea is really important?'

'Vital!' he said. 'OH, YOGHURTS!' he yelled as he saw what I was getting at. 'Floatie is still stuck in Stewart Road. I haven't done half my round, have I?'

I wondered when he would remember.

'What am I going to do?'

I held up my hoof and told him to calm down. There was a simple solution . . . me!

He looked into my eyes and blinked. 'You,' he said, sounding really surprised.

'Well, I have been doing the job for the past twenty years; one more day won't hurt. I was retired all of yesterday so I've had a good rest. Now, go and get the harness, drag the old cart out from behind the stable and let's go and get the milk.'

He didn't need to be told twice. He galloped off, his chubby little legs a blur. Moments later he came back with my old leather collar. As he slipped it over my head, it felt cold and hard at first but I soon snuggled into it. Next he led me into the forks of the cart and started to strap me in. I heard the familiar creak of the old springs as he climbed back into the driving seat and picked up the reins. 'Come on then, old boy,' he said. 'One more time.'

It was great to get out on the road again. I know it had only been a day but I had already started to miss the sights and sounds. You see, I know everyone and everyone knows me. As we clip-clopped down Brynteg Lane, people came out to say hello. As we swung into James Street, children

waved from the windows. Then left into Stewart Road where a small crowd had gathered around Floatie.

As we pulled up, everybody clapped, and patted me. 'We knew he would get you out again,' said Mr Jones from Number Thirty.

'Good to have you back,' said Mr Williams from the paper shop.

Mike started to sort out the orders, something that he was never very good at, but the crowd in Stewart Road reminded him of what they wanted and soon everybody was happy and walking back to their breakfast tables with pints of milk, cartons of juice and packets of butter.

We looked at Floatie.

'Not a spark of life,' said Mike, pulling switches and pressing buttons. 'Let's get the crates off, finish the round and then we'll get back and call the garage.'

Chapter Seven

Caitlin Avenue is long, with lots of houses and, to be honest, if it wasn't for me, I don't know how Mike would remember who got what. He always had particular trouble remembering the orders for the first three families as they were all called Davies.

We pulled up at Number One. 'Right,' he said. 'Miss Davies, a pint and some cream. Or is that Mrs Davies at Number Two?' He scratched his moustache and fiddled with the reins.

'No, Mrs Davies lives at Number Three,' I reminded him. 'Mr Davies, that's Dai Davies, is at Number Two: he has a yoghurt, a pint and a carton of juice.'

'How can you remember that?' said Mike, jumping down from the cart.

'It's simple. I have a little rhyme for the houses and the orders.'

Mike looked at me as if I was mad.

'Look . . . it's so easy. Let's start at Number One Caitlin Avenue: Miss Davies. The rhyme is, *three pints full-fat . . . and cream for the cat.* You remember, she has that horrible fat ginger thing called Terrance. She spoils it rotten.'

Mike nodded. 'Oh, yes. It's the size of a dustbin; clawed my trousers last Christmas.'

'That's it. So remember, *three pints full-fat . . . and cream for the cat.* Now, Number Two is Dai Davies in the really shabby house. The gate is always hanging off its hinges. So I always say . . . *a yoghurt, a pint and a carton of juice, up to the house where the dog is loose.* His Jack Russell is always getting out of the gate.'

Mike's eyes lit up. 'That's brilliant!'

'And now to Number Three . . . Mrs Davies . . . that's Mrs Rhys Davies to be exact; she's about to go on holiday and needs to get into her swimming costume. Although if you ask me, they'll be lucky to get her into the plane!'

Mike giggled. 'What's the rhyme?'

'Mavis Rhys Davies, just one pint of skimmed; she's going to Spain and she needs to be slimmed.'

'That's marvellous,' he said. 'You're a genius.'

I puffed out my chest. 'I'm not just a pretty face. Floatie may be modern but I can remember the orders, and I know the route like the back of my hoof.'

Mike got out a notebook and pencil. 'OK, let's see if I have this right. I'll just take it down so I can look at it tonight.'

'Good idea,' I said. 'Off you go, take it slowly, and remember the rhymes.'

Mike closed his eyes and said, 'Mavis Rhys Davies is terribly fat, two pints and a yoghurt and a semi-skinned cat.'

'No,' I said. 'No, that's not it at all: *Mavis Rhys Davies, just one pint of skimmed; she's going to Spain and she needs to be slimmed.* And that's house Number Three. What about house Number Two?'

'OK. Mr Davies with the gate that is loose. A yoghurt, a pint and some juice for the moose!'

'No, *a yoghurt, a pint and a carton of juice, up to the house where the dog is loose.* He's got a Jack Russell, not a moose.' I gave Mike one of my dark looks. 'You can't keep a moose in Caitlin Avenue,' I said. 'It's one-way for a start! And what about Miss Davies at Number One? You've missed her out altogether. *Three pints full-fat and cream for the cat.*'

He gave me a broad grin. 'Oh yes, the cat she spoils rotten. I'd totally forgotten!'

'Well "rotten" rhymes with "forgotten", I suppose, so it's a start.' I shuffled my hooves. 'Let's get the deliveries done and I will go through the rhymes with you again on the way back to the yard.'

He sighed, put his notebook away and climbed on board.

It must have been near nine o'clock when we got back to the St Mary Dairy in Pont-y-cary. Mike had muttered all the way home about semi-skinned cats and a moose on the loose.

We parked the cart and I slipped out of my harness; Mike rubbed me down and poured me a large, refreshing bucket of water. He went into the house for a big pot of tea, but not before I reminded him to ring the garage. Later on, he came back out with his notebook and I helped him to make a list of all the orders. I had rhymes for them all, all the families in Stewart Road, Brynteg Lane and James Street, all the shops and all the factories.

It was nearly midday when Cardigan popped his head over the door. 'I thought you'd retired?' he said.

'I had. And if I am lucky . . . I might retire again – tomorrow!'

I fluffed up my straw and lay down beside Rhodri and Rhys who were still fast asleep. Flight Lieutenant Pigeon was snoring in the rafters above my head and I could hear the ducklings quacking about on the pond. It was good to be home and great to be the last horse in Wales to pull a milk cart.

But, between ourselves,

I don't think my job is finished yet.

Do you?